BBC toybox
Treasury

ISBN 0 563 38083 7

Published by BBC Worldwide Ltd
Woodlands, 80 Wood Lane, London W12 OTT

First published 1998
This presentation copyright © BBC Worldwide Ltd 1998

Typeset by BBC Worldwide Ltd
Colour separations by Dot Gradations Ltd
Printed by Cambus Litho Ltd, East Kilbride
Bound by Hunter and Foulis Ltd, Edinburgh

Contents

Pingu Does the Housework

All was quiet in Pingu's house. Mum was hard at work ironing. She looked up and sighed wearily. The house was in a terrible mess.

"Come and help me, Pingu," she called. "I've got such a lot of housework to be getting on with."

"Why can't Pinga help you?" groaned Pingu, busy reading his book. "She's only playing with her toys."

"Oh, yes please, Mum," said Pinga. "I love helping." Pinga picked up the pile of clothes Mum had just ironed.

On her way over to the cupboard Pinga dropped some of the clothes.

"I've just washed and ironed those and now they're all dirty and crumpled again," snapped Mum.

Pinga burst into tears. "I was only trying to help," she sobbed.

"I'm sorry I was cross," said Mum gently. "It's not your fault. I am just so tired today. Pingu, you're bigger than Pinga and you'll just have to help me."

Pingu balanced a large pile of clothes on his head and danced his way over to the cupboard.

"You can clean the floor now," said Mum and gave Pingu a bucket of soapy water.

Suddenly Pingu began to cheer up. While Mum's back was turned he tipped lots more soap powder into the water. The bucket filled with bubbles.

"Yippee!" cried Pinga. "I love bubbles!"

"Good!" laughed Pingu as he plopped a huge handful of them on her head.

Mum rubbed the bubbles off Pinga's head. "Stop being silly and just get on with the cleaning, Pingu," she said in a tired voice.

Pingu started to clean the floor. Pinga decided to join
in. But when she lifted up the broom she knocked a
clean bedspread right into the bucket of soapy water.

"Oh, no!" she cried, fishing out the wet bedspread.
"What will Mum say?" She took the bedspread over
to the oven and popped it inside. "It should dry
quickly in there," she said.

Meanwhile Pingu was helping Mum finish the
housework. She was very grateful. As soon as the
house was tidy it was time for Mum to make supper.

Just then Dad came back from work.

Dad gave Mum a kiss. "Have you had a good day?" he asked.

"I've been very busy with the housework," said Mum. "But Pingu has helped me."

Pingu puffed himself out proudly. "I worked very hard," he told Dad.

"Supper is nearly ready," said Mum as she opened the door of the oven. Mum was very shocked to find her best bedspread cooking away inside it.

"What is that doing in here?" she exclaimed. "It could have caught fire and burnt the house down!"

"I didn't put it in there, honestly," cried Pingu. "I know how dangerous that could be."

Pinga hid nervously behind her brother. Pingu went up to the bedspread and hugged it.

"Mmmm," he said. "It feels lovely and warm. Can we have it in our bed tonight?"

That night, Pingu and Pinga were tucked up in bed under the baked bedspread.

"You shouldn't have put it in the oven, Pinga, but I do like it better warmed through!," said Pingu. "Anyway, after all the housework I've done today I could fall asleep under anything!"

William and the Genie

One night William couldn't get to sleep. He kept thinking about the genie in his bedtime story. A wicked king had stolen his magic lamp and now the genie had nowhere to live.

William decided to go and visit the genie and see if he could help him find his lamp again. He made a wish with his magic wellingtons and soon he was flying through the sky on an enchanted quilt.

Before long he came to a mysterious cave with a big, gaping mouth.

William flew straight into the cave.

"I wonder where the genie is," he said.

"I'm stuck up here," cried a miserable voice. "I've lost my lamp and I've nowhere else to go."

"I'll help you get your lamp back," said William.

William took the genie to the King's palace on his flying quilt. They crept inside the palace and peeped into the royal bedroom. There they saw the King reading in bed with the genie's lamp beside him.

The King looked rather cross.

William bravely stepped out of his hiding place.

"What's wrong, your Majesty?" asked William.

The King explained that the lamp wasn't bright enough for him to read by.

So William made a wish and a smart bedside lamp appeared.

"Would you swap your lamp for this lovely new one?" asked William.

The King thought that was a very good idea and gave William the genie's lamp back.

The genie was happy too. "Thank you!" he cried, as he slid back inside his old lamp.

"Magic lamps are all very well," thought William as he wished himself home, "but they're not as good as wish wellingtons!"

Fireman Sam and Naughty Norman

It was Fireman Sam's day off. "I think I'll give that old fence a new coat of paint," decided Sam.

He went off to Pontypandy to buy some paint. Then he carried it into the garden.

As Sam got down to work, he heard a bang behind him and felt something whizz past!

A ball had flown over the fence and knocked the paintbrush out of his hand!

Sam bent down to pick up the ball. Then he spotted Naughty Norman Price peering over the other side of the fence.

"That naughty boy," thought Sam. "He must have thrown the ball over and knocked the paint brush out of my hand."

Sam had an idea.

Sam called Naughty Norman over into his garden.
"Look at my window, Norman!" said Sam angrily.
"When you threw your ball over the fence it
smashed into it and left a large hole."

"I'm very sorry Sam," said Naughty Norman,
looking alarmed. "I didn't mean to break it. Is there
anything I can do to help?"

"Hmm," said Sam, "let me see. Well my old fence
does need a new coat of paint."

Norman offered to paint Sam's fence. He felt very guilty for breaking Fireman Sam's window.

Sam relaxed in the sunshine, gently rocking backwards and forwards in his garden chair. He smiled to himself as he thought about the surprise he had for Norman.

Norman painted the fence a new bright blue colour as quickly as he could. He was beginning to feel quite hungry and tired. The fence was very big!

Naughty Norman finally finished painting the last panel of the fence. He was exhausted!

Sam called Norman to the broken window. He picked up a damp cloth and began to wipe the hole. The hole disappeared!

Norman was amazed. The window was not broken after all.

"I painted a hole onto the glass," laughed Sam. "I wanted to teach you a lesson!"

Sam had made a special tea for Naughty Norman to say thank you for painting his fence.

Sam and Norman sat by the kitchen window eating chocolate rolls and jelly. They admired the newly painted fence.

"This is really great," laughed Norman, tucking into his third chocolate roll. "Are there any more jobs I can do?!"

Dinobabies and the Flying Lesson

The Dinobabies were all playing Hunt-the-Treecrab. Marshall had seen a treecrab go up a tall tree, and he had sent his big brother, Franklin, up to catch it.

"I've got it!" yelled Franklin, leaning out of the tree to show Marshall the treecrab. But then he noticed how high up he was. "Help! I'm scared of heights! I can't move!"

The other Dinobabies came running towards the cries.

Dak flew up to the top of the tree. "What's wrong?" he asked.

24

"I'm scared," said Franklin. "I can't get down."

"Grab hold of my foot," said Dak, and he flew down to the ground with Franklin.

"Did you get the treecrab?" asked Marshall.

"No, I forgot it because I was scared," said Franklin.

"You've ruined the game, Franklin," said Marshall sadly, and he turned away.

"I wish I wasn't scared of heights," said Franklin. "Then Marshall would be proud of me."

"Well, maybe you should learn to fly like Dak," said Stanley. "And I've got an idea how you could learn. Come over here."

Stanley made Franklin sit in a very springy tree, and catapulted him into the air.

"Hey, look at me! I'm flying!" shouted Franklin. "No I'm not – I'm falling!" he cried, and he dropped all the way down on to a giant mushroom.

"I've got another idea," said Stanley. He took Franklin to the top of a cliff and gave him two big palm leaves for wings. Marshall made him a pointy beak out of another leaf.

Just then, Dak flew up to see what was going on.

"Franklin's not smart enough to fly," laughed Dak.

"I am!" shouted Franklin, and he jumped high into the air. But he couldn't fly!

"He-e-eelp!" he cried, as he fell faster and faster.

"Grab my feet," shouted Dak, coming to the rescue.

"I can't. My wings are in the way," cried Franklin, and he started to shake them off. But as he shook his wings harder and harder, he stopped falling. And soon, he was flying.

"Look! I can fly!" shouted Franklin. "I can fly!"

"We can play some great games now," said Dak.

"This game is fun," said Dak. "Grab some gooey, squashy melons and follow me."

Franklin grabbed a melon in each hand and flew after Dak.

Dak and Franklin flew over the other Dinobabies and dropped the gooey, squashy melons on their heads! Then they flew away, laughing.

"I'm not going to forget this," said LaBrea, angrily.

"There's one very fun game my mum said I couldn't play anymore . . . but *you* could play it!," Dak said to Franklin. "Come on, let's find a T-Rex. This is the best game of all."

"Wrap this vine round and round the T-Rex," giggled Dak. "It'll take it ages to break free."

"That sounds like fun," said Franklin. He flew over the T-Rex and wound the vine round his arms and head.

"Ha, ha!" laughed Franklin, as the T-Rex started to
roar. But just then, one of Franklin's leaf wings
broke in two, and he fell into a bush.

"Help! Help me!" cried Franklin, as the T-Rex broke
free of the vine. "Dak, help me!" shouted Franklin.
"I'm stuck in this bush!"

"Erm, I've got to go now," said Dak, "See you
later."

"Help me! Help!" screamed Franklin, as the T-Rex
drew closer.

Just in time, the other Dinobabies heard his cries
and they came and pulled him out of the bush.

Luckily the Dinobabies managed to escape from the angry T-Rex.

"Thanks for helping me," said Franklin. "I'm never ever going to fly again, not after that. It was really scary."

"Well," said Truman, "There's something waiting at the treecave you should be scared of, too."

"What's that?" asked Franklin.

"ME!" shouted LaBrea. She hadn't forgotten about the gooey, squashy melon that had landed on her head!

Noddy and the Useful Rope

One afternoon Noddy was polishing his car when Mr Tubby arrived.

"I meant to throw this rope away, but I thought you might like it for your car, Noddy?" asked Mr Tubby.

"Thank you very much, Mr Tubby," said Noddy. "I'm sure it will be very useful to have a rope."

Noddy got in his car and drove to the cafe. Mr Jumbo was waiting for Noddy to pick him up and take him to the station.

When they arrived at the station, Mr Jumbo asked Noddy to collect him from the evening train. Dinah Doll greeted Noddy.

"I am glad that you're here," she said. "Please could you take me into town. I've got this huge crate full of books to sell on my stall, and it's very heavy."

"Yes, of course I will help," said Noddy. "I know, I can tie this rope that Mr Tubby Bear gave me around the crate and drag it to my car. I knew this would be a useful rope!"

Noddy and Dinah Doll drove off into town.

Tessie Bear and Mr Wobbly Man were looking after
Dinah Doll's stand until she got back from the station.

Noddy and Dinah arrived in the car and began
pushing the heavy crate towards Dinah Doll's stall!

"Excuse me," cried Mr Wobbly Man. "I don't wish to
be any trouble, but I appear to be stuck between this
huge crate and Dinah Doll's stall!"

Noddy had squashed poor Mr Wobbly Man between
the crate and the stall!

"We need a rope to pull him out," said Tessie Bear.

"I've got a very useful rope!" cried Noddy.

Noddy tied one end of the rope around Mr Wobbly
Man, and the other end to his car. Noddy started up
the engine and his little car pulled as hard as it could.

All of a sudden, Mr Wobbly Man shot up into the air and landed safely on top of the crate.

"Well done, Noddy," said Tessie. "Thank you for all your help."

That evening, Noddy picked up Mr Jumbo from the station and brought him home. He took Mr Jumbo's luggage out of his car and put it outside his house. But when he turned round, his car had started to move slowly away down the road.

"Oh no!" cried Noddy. "My car!"

Mr Jumbo quickly grabbed hold of the rope which was still trailing from the back of Noddy's car.

"You should tie it to the lamppost," said Mr Jumbo.

"Thank you, Mr Jumbo," said Noddy. "I will – I'll use my useful rope to keep my car still while we take out the rest of your luggage."

"Thank you, Noddy," said Mr Jumbo. "You have been very helpful."

"Goodnight, Mr Jumbo," said Noddy and he started to drive away. But he didn't realise that the car was still tied to the lamppost!

As Noddy drove through Toy Town, he could hear a loud clattering noise. Noddy drove past Mr Plod. The lamppost knocked Mr Plod right over! Noddy stopped the car immediately.

"What do you think you're doing towing a lamppost along at night?" Mr Plod asked sternly.

"Good gracious!" exclaimed Noddy. "It's the lamppost from Mr Jumbo's house. Oh dear! My car started to roll away, so I had to tie it to the nearest lamppost with my useful rope!"

Noddy and Mr Plod went back to Mr Jumbo's house.
Mr Jumbo was standing outside.

"I felt it was my duty to stand here with my torch
until help arrived," exclaimed Mr Jumbo.

"Thank you Mr Jumbo," said Mr Plod and Noddy
drove him back to the police station.

Mr Plod suddenly had a thought.

"Noddy, you still haven't untied that lamppost!"

"You didn't remind me to," grinned Noddy.

"Oh bother! I suppose that means I am as
forgetful as you are!" said Mr Plod.

"Yes you are!" laughed Noddy. "Never mind,
Mr Plod. It really is a very useful rope!"

Pingu and the Spotty Day

One morning Pingu was painting a picture and Pinga was crawling around on the floor when the phone rang. Before Mum could get to it, Pinga had answered it herself by sitting on Pingu's shoulders.

Mum came over and took the phone from Pinga. It was Grandpa.

"Oh dear!" she exclaimed. "Spots, you say? I am sorry. We'll come straight over." And she put down the phone.

"Grandpa's ill," she told Pingu and Pinga. "We must go and look after him."

They all rode off to Grandpa's house in the post truck. They found Grandpa looking very sorry for himself.

"Don't come too near me," he said. "I'm covered in spots and I wouldn't want you to catch anything."

"Grandpa is right," said Mum. "And please be quiet because he needs all the rest he can get."

Pingu didn't like not being able to say hello properly to Grandpa, so he took his walking stick and held it out for him to shake.

Mum went off to make some hot soup for Grandpa. Pingu and Pinga began to run round and round Grandpa's armchair. They squealed and hooted.

Grandpa held his head in his hands. "I can't take all this noise," he groaned.

Mum was furious with Pingu and Pinga. "I told you I didn't want any trouble from you. Grandpa is feeling very poorly. Now go and find something quiet to do."

Pingu and Pinga decided to explore Grandpa's cupboard. Pinga found an old top hat and Pingu slid round the room. Then Pingu crashed into the cupboard and everything fell out of it.

"Oh my poor head!" moaned Grandpa. "This is too much."

Mum had had enough.

"Go outside," she shouted. "I don't want to hear another squeak out of you until we go home."

Pingu and Pinga began to play football outside. Pingu was kicking snowballs into the goal. Pinga was trying to stop them.

"Goal! Goal! Goal!" Pingu shouted out gleefully each time a snowball hit the door. Just as Pingu had another shot at the goal, Mum opened the door. SPLOSH – the snowball landed right in Mum's face.

"Goal!" yelled Pingu and started to giggle. But neither Pingu nor Pinga giggled for long. They had never seen Mum look so cross.

"Go straight home," she ordered. "You've done nothing but make a noise all morning. You're two extremely naughty penguins."

Back at home Pingu and Pinga were feeling a bit guilty for making so much noise.

"Poor old Grandpa," said Pinga. "But he did look funny with spots!"

Then Pingu had an idea. He got out his crayons and began to draw spots on himself. Pinga laughed and drew spots on her face too.

"I know how to stop Mum from being cross with us," said Pingu. He went over to the telephone.

At Grandpa's house, Mum was rubbing some soothing cream on Grandpa's spots when the phone rang. It was Pingu.

"I'm afraid Pingu and Pinga have come out in spots," Mum told Grandpa worriedly. "I'll have to go home and look after them."

Mum rushed home as fast as she could. She found the two penguins in bed.

"Oh, you poor things," said Mum, stroking Pingu's head.

Then she looked at her hand. It was covered in crayon. She couldn't understand it. She looked at Pingu's head where she had stroked him. The spots were smeared together and were now just a mess of crayon.

Pingu and Pinga started to laugh and Mum joined in.

Mum was so relieved that Pingu and Pinga weren't really ill that she couldn't be cross with them. She even let Pingu draw spots on her head!

"We might as well all be spotty together," she said. For the first time that day Mum was enjoying herself. She jumped onto Pingu's bed and they all gave each other a hug.

William and the Detective

One day William and his mother came home from the shops. They couldn't find the front door key anywhere.

"Where could I have put it?" wondered Mum.

"I wish I was a great detective," wished William. "Then I could find it."

William put on his wellingtons and made a wish!
His wish came true!

"Now all we need is a big mystery to solve," said
Sherlock William to Doctor Barksure.

At that very moment a carriage drew up. Inside
was a Duchess who needed Sherlock William's help.

"At your service, Duchess," said William, politely.

The Duchess took Sherlock William and Doctor Barksure back to her enormous house where she explained the mystery.

"Last night while I was dining, the candles mysteriously blew out. When we lit them again, I discovered that all my silver had disappeared!" she said.

"Doctor Barksure will track your thief down," said Sherlock William.

Barksure sniffed around the room and then shot out into the garden where he followed the thief's trail to the foot of a tall tree.

"Stranger and stranger!" said William. "Doctor Barksure thinks the thief is in the tree."

Suddenly, from one of the branches tumbled a nest full of the duchess's silver, followed by a sheepish magpie.

The Duchess was delighted to have her treasures back.

"Don't worry, I'm not cross with you," she said to the magpie. "I know that magpies love shiny things."

The magpie promised not to steal her silver again.

The Duchess thanked Sherlock William and Doctor Barksure and waved goodbye.

Back at home, William felt something inside his boot. It was the door key.

"You've found it," said Mum. "Well done, William."

"Another mystery solved," he grinned. "It's elementary when you've got a pair of magic wish wellingtons!"

Fireman Sam and the Windy Day

It was a windy day and leaves were being blown off the trees all over Pontypandy. There were piles of leaves everywhere in Officer Steele's garden, and soggy leaves were covering Pontypandy fire station.

"We must do something about these leaves," said Sam. He decided to telephone the twins to ask for their help.

Sarah and James came round and swept up the yard. Then they helped Sam wash Jupiter.

"There are an awful lot of leaves everywhere Sam!" said Sarah.

"No sooner have we swept up, then lots more leaves blow down from the trees again," said Sam, peeling a wet leaf from his helmet.

Sarah and James finished washing Jupiter. He was now clean and shiny and didn't have one leaf on him!

"Thank you for your help Sarah and James," said Fireman Sam.

Sarah and James had worked so hard clearing all the leaves from the yard, they were now very hungry. It was time for tea!

On their way home Sarah thought she could smell smoke.

"Look!" shouted James. "Officer Steele's house!"

Sarah and James could see a funnel of smoke rising out of Officer Steele's house.

"Quick," shouted James. "We must call the Fire Station."

Sarah ran to the nearest phone to call Fireman Sam.

"Sam, please come quickly," cried Sarah.

Fireman Sam jumped into Jupiter and raced down the street, sending leaves scattering everywhere.

Meanwhile Sarah and James quickly ran over to Officer Steele's house. They arrived at exactly the same time as Sam screeched round the corner in Jupiter.

Fireman Sam ran into Officer Steele's back garden. Sarah and James followed closely behind.

But Officer Steele's house wasn't on fire – he was just burning the leaves in his garden! Whilst Sam had been clearing the yard at the Fire Station, Officer Steele had decided to get rid of all the leaves that had settled in his back garden.

"Well done Sarah and James for acting so quickly!" said Officer Steele. "It could easily have been a real fire."

"Well done Sarah and James," said Fireman Sam. "Sorry for disturbing you Officer Steele!"

Fireman Sam then noticed Jupiter.

"Jupiter's all covered in leaves again!" said Sam.

"Never mind," laughed Officer Steele. "I think we have all worked so hard that we deserve a nice hot cup of tea and a slice of ginger cake! Come inside!"

Sarah and James quickly ran into Officer Steele's house – they were still very hungry!

Dinobabies and the Monsters

One day, the Dinobabies were playing in their treecave when they heard a loud tumbling noise. The ground began to shake.

"An earthquake," yelled Franklin. "Abandon treecave!"

The Dinobabies rushed outside and watched in horror as the whole treecave fell down.

"All our hard work has been ruined," said Stanley. "I'm going to find out how much damage there is. Follow me."

The Dinobabies followed Stanley though the woods until he suddenly tumbled down a huge crack in the ground.

The Dinobabies decided to follow Stanley down into the large hole. "Wait for us!" they cried.

"Let's go this way," said Stanley, looking around. They had fallen into a big cave with lots of tunnels.

But after a while, the Dinobabies realised that they were completely lost.

"I think we'd better shout for help," advised Truman.

"HELP! We're lost," shrieked the Dinobabies.

Suddenly, three little creatures popped up from behind a pile of rocks.

"We'll help you," they said.

"Aaaargh!" screamed the Dinobabies. "Monsters!"

The three little creatures laughed. "We're not monsters," they giggled. "We're gargoyles and we live here. We'll show you the way out if you follow us."

"No thanks," chorused the Dinobabies. "You look scary and strange. We'll find our own way out."

"Don't go that way," said one of the gargoyles. "You'll get into trouble."

"We don't believe you," said Dak, and he led the Dinobabies off down the tunnel.

Suddenly Dak, Franklin, Truman, Stanley and LaBrea all fell into an underground stream.

"Wow-oow!" they yelled as they were swept away.

"I think I'll go back and ask the gargoyles for help," said Marshall, wisely.

The gargoyles were very kind and they showed Marshall the way back up.

"Thanks," said Marshall. "You're not scary or strange at all. I think you're nice. Come up and play."

"Is it safe?," asked the gargoyles. "Aren't there lots of monsters up there?"

"Of course it's safe," said Marshall. "Come and see our treecave." But when they arrived it was covered in rubble. Marshall had forgotten that the earthquake ruined it.

"We'll help rebuild it for you," offered the gargoyles.

Meanwhile, the other Dinobabies were having a bad time. Covered in mud, they scrambled out of the stream.

"Run," they screamed, heading for the light.

Eventually, they found their way out of the pit. Exhausted, the Dinobabies made their way back to the treecave.

They couldn't believe their eyes when they saw it had been rebuilt.

"The treecave's back!" cried Franklin. "And there's Marshall!"

"The gargoyles brought me home and rebuilt the treecave," said Marshall.

"Thank you gargoyles," chorused the Dinobabies. "We're sorry we didn't trust you just because you look different," said LaBrea.

"That's all right," said the gargoyles. "We really enjoyed helping Marshall rebuild the treecave. But we've got to go now. It's dinner time and all the crunchy cockroaches will be out."

"Yuk!" said Stanley. "We may be friends now, but I don't think we'll ever come to dinner with you!"

Noddy Delivers Some Parcels

It was a rather busy morning for Noddy. It was Big-Ear's birthday, and Noddy began baking him a very special cake.

"I've got so much to do," Noddy thought to himself. "I have to buy Big-Ears a present, but I haven't enough money yet. I shall put the cake in the oven now, and drive into Toy Town to see if I can earn sixpence. Then I can buy Big-Ears a brand new cocoa mug with toadstools on it."

Noddy was in luck!

"Noddy!" cried Pink Cat, as he drove past her house. "I want you to take this parcel to the station, and collect another box which is waiting for me there. It contains my beautiful new teaset. I will pay you two sixpences when you get back."

"This parcel hasn't even got any string round it," said Noddy crossly.

Noddy went to buy some string from Dinah Doll.

"I have to take this parcel to the station for Pink Cat," said Noddy. "Then I can buy a cocoa mug with toadstools on it for Big-Ears."

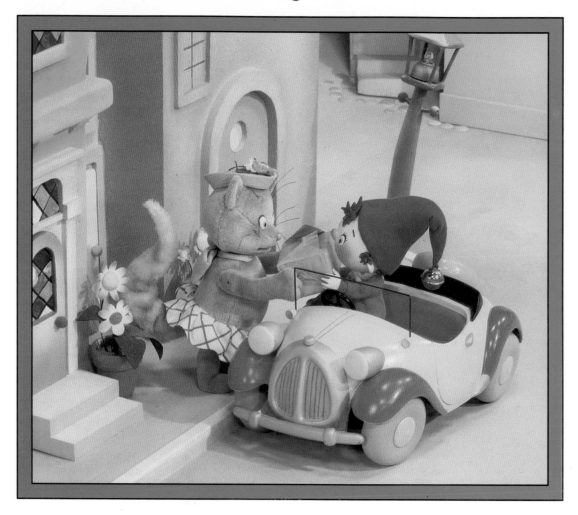

"I've sold out of cocoa mugs!" said Dinah Doll.
"But if you collect a parcel for me at the station, I
shall have some more."

Noddy drove to the station.

"Oh Mr Driver! I'm glad you're still here," said
Noddy breathlessly. Pink Cat asked me to give you
this parcel. Do you have any boxes here for Pink Cat
and Dinah Doll?"

"Yes, they are over here. I'm afraid the labels got
rather smudged in the rain," explained Mr Driver.

Noddy decided the smaller parcel must be for Pink Cat.

"Tea cups are much smaller than mugs," he said and he dropped the small parcel off at Pink Cat's house. Noddy drove off to Dinah Doll's stall.

As Noddy gave Dinah Doll her parcel, he suddenly remembered Big-Ear's other surprise back at House-for-One.

"The cake! I left it in the oven! I must go!" he cried, and rushed off.

Meanwhile, Dinah started to unpack her box.

"Good gracious!" she said. "This isn't a box of cocoa mugs with toadstools on them. This is a beautiful china tea-set!"

Meanwhile, Noddy was running into his house to rescue the cake.

"Oh dear," he said. "I do hope it will taste all right. It smells . . . er . . . very smelly. I think I should take it out of the oven straight away."

Just then, there came a knock on the door.

"Oh dear!" said Noddy again. "Come in!"

"Now Noddy," said Mr Plod, sternly. "What have you done with Miss Pink Cat's tea-set?"

"I've delivered it to her," said Noddy.

"Well, Miss Pink Cat says she hasn't got it. You'd better come with me and sort this out," said Mr Plod.

Noddy followed Mr Plod out of the house, completely forgetting about the cake.

Pink Cat was looking at the tea-set on Dinah Doll's stall. "I can't sell this one to you," said Dinah. "It's not mine. Noddy delivered it to me by mistake."

"He brought me a horrible set of cocoa mugs with toadstools on them," said Pink Cat.

"So *that's* what happened to my parcel," said Dinah.

When Noddy and Mr Plod arrived, Dinah Doll explained that Noddy had muddled up the parcels.

"Well, now we have sorted that out shall we go and celebrate Big-Ear's birthday?" said Mr Plod.

All Big-Ear's friends gathered at Noddy's house to see Big-Ears open his presents. Everyone had bought him cocoa mugs with toadstools on!

"Oh!" cried Noddy. "I've just remembered . . ." He took the cake out of the oven. It was burnt to a cinder.

"I'm so sorry, Big-Ears!" said Noddy. "Now you won't have a birthday cake."

Just then Mr and Mrs Tubby Bear walked in holding a beautiful birthday cake on it for Big Ears! "Happy Birthday, Big-Ears!" they all cried.

"Thank you everyone" laughed Big Ears.

You can now enjoy all your favourite
characters in Toybox books, audio tapes and
videos and every month in Toybox Magazine